ON

CW01661986

ONCE UPON A MONDAY

• • •

SAM UMUKORO

Copyright © Sam Umukoro 2021

The moral right of Sam Umukoro to be identified as the Author of this work has been asserted by him in accordance with the Copyright, Designs, and Patents Act 1988.

ISBN: 978-1-7399838-0-2

All rights reserved.

No part of this book may be reproduced, stored in a retrieval system, or transported in any form or by any means (electronic, mechanical, photocopying, recording or otherwise), without the prior written permission of the publisher of this book.

This is a work of fiction. Names, characters, businesses, places, and incidents are either the product of the author's imagination or are used fictitiously. Any resemblance to actual persons, living or dead, events or locales is entirely coincidental.

First published in 2002 by **Epik Books**

This edition is published by

Nufora Company

Wolverhampton

West Midlands

United Kingdom

Email: contact@nuforacompany.com

Cover Design and Layout by Shobola Ibukun

For Dean and Helen

ONCE UPON A MONDAY

I woke up on Monday with Becky on my mind. Words could not describe how much I missed her. The love we shared meant the world to me.

I met Becky on a Monday morning. It was love at first sight. Ironically, it was on a Monday that I lost her. The day began like any other day with brilliant sunshine, trees resplendent in green leaves, blowing gently in the wind in a cloudless sky. Nothing in the seemingly perfect morning warned us that fanatics were going to dance naked in the market place and stalk the streets like ravenous lions in search of prey. I should not have not allowed Becky out of my sight, but how could I have foreseen that we would be victims of religious fanatics. How could I have known we would fall victim to their violent depredations.

I was sitting in front of my house when I saw my younger brother, Atimas, running down the street towards me as if a thousand demons were hot on his heels.

"What is the matter?" I asked as soon as he got to where I was seated.

"The...riot...has...started," he panted, his eyes wide with fear. "They are killing people in town!" he blurted out.

"And where is Becky?" I asked.

"I don't know. We were separated when the fanatics attacked the bus we were riding in."

Cold dread closed iron fingers around my throat. I quickly rushed into the house, picked up my dagger and stepped out.

Atimas held on to the tail of my shirt. "Ple...a...se don't go, Balat," he pleaded. "They will kill you."

"No! I must look for Becky, we can't abandon her. Where did you say your bus was attacked?"

"Around Kawo bus stop." It was not too far away from our house.

The city was already a mesh of rubble, ashes, blood and scattered limbs: life had become cheap like a sachet of 'pure water' on the streets of Lagos.

The violence was still raging. People were running helter-skelter, there was confusion everywhere. Our city had become an ironic metaphor reminiscent of the song by Fela, "Sorrow, tears and blood..."

I sought frantically for Becky. I couldn't find her around Kawo bus stop. At the General Hospital popularly called 'Asibiti': there were at least thirty corpses deposited in front of the mortuary there. Some of the bodies were charred, others badly mutilated with marks of violence. I inspected the bodies but thankfully she was not there. I moved through the wards carefully, but still did not find her. I continued to worry about what could have happened to her.

I was really getting frantic and cautioned myself that I was searching for Becky in the wrong place. I decided to return home before I came to harm myself. I took the back streets to avoid the orgy of bloodletting, destruction and anarchy in the major streets. As I got to a street corner, a familiar voice called my name. My heart did a double somersault as I turned to see who it was: it was Dikko, one of my childhood friends. I quickly ran to where he stood.

"Have you seen Becky?"

"No, Balat. Don't go home yet. The fanatics are on their way to your street!"

"I must leave now, I left Atimas alone at home. I must rush back to him." Just then, Dikko and I saw the fanatics coming in our direction. They were brandishing dangerous weapons. We took to our heels and hid in a deserted building.

Fortunately, they didn't come after us. From hiding, we watched with horror as our neighbours were dragged out of their houses and hacked to death. We were so shocked by the gory sight before us that we didn't notice that Musa, the popular madman in town, had also taken refuge in the building with us. It was his cough that alerted us. Dikko and I clung to each other in fright. But our fear was quickly dissolved when we saw the mischievous smile planted on his face. Clearly for Musa the riot was some kind of vindication: we, the so-called 'sane ones', were actually the 'insane ones'.

Musa the madman was more popular than the Governor of the state. The story of his madness has become folklore.

Some people believed that Musa's madness started in his student days at the Ahmadu Bello University, Zaria. According to them, Musa was a very brilliant young man who, in his first year as a mathematics student, was already solving mathematical problems for students ahead of him in the department. Even the professors in his department consulted him about mathematical problems they couldn't solve. This earned him the sobriquet 'Professor Musa Emeritus'. Musa's reputation spread far and wide on campus to the extent that that many other students from other departments like Civil Engineering, Mechanical Engineering and Physics brought all sorts of mathematical equations for him to solve. It didn't take long for the University Senate to notice him. In his second year, the Senate sat and decided that, since Musa was very brilliant and already teaching professors, the university should award him accelerated promotion and a First-Class degree without him meeting the mandatory requirement of spending four years of study, but only on condition that he must solve a mathematical problem that professors in the university, dead or alive, had never been able to solve.

When he was given the equation, Musa applied himself diligently to the task. For days on end, he stayed in his room trying to solve the equation. The news spread around the campus that 'Professor Musa Emeritus' was trying to solve a mathematical equation that no professor dead or alive had been able to unravel. Many students kept vigil outside his room; some set up canopies in front of his hostel. No one wanted to miss the historic moment when Musa announced to the school authorities and the world that he had solved the equation. Entrepreneurs on campus made brisk business; they printed Musa's face on t-shirts and caps, and sold the merchandise to the students. With bated breath, they all waited for Musa to come out of his room with the answer.

After forty days and forty nights, Musa came out. He stared at the mass of people in front of him for a moment and then burst into hysterical laughter. The crowd cheered, thinking that Musa's laughter was an indication of his success at solving the mathematical equation. "Long live Professor Musa Emeritus!" some hailed from the crowd. Musa's next move took the crowd by surprise. He took off his clothes till he was completely naked and started screaming: "You can't get me! You can't get me! I am like Mandela, triumphant from Robben Island. Yes, I am Chaka the Zulu, with many vassal states under my rule. I am Mai Idris Alooma, visionary leader of Kanem-Bornu Empire. I am Jaja of Opobo, resisting colonialism. I reign like Mansa Musa of the Mali Empire in splendour and wealth. Yes, I am a strong warrior from Africa, you can't get me!"

It took some time for the crowd to realize that Musa had gone crazy. Pandemonium broke out, the school security men were alerted, and he was whisked away to the school's Teaching Hospital, where doctors certified him insane. The general opinion was that the mathematical problem drove Musa round the bend.

Another account has it that, before he became mad, Musa was a top security goon for my country's late dictator who died of suspected poisoning after eating an exotic fruit from the Far-East. Musa was rumoured to have carried out dastardly acts for the late dictator. The late dictator loved him for his bravery and loyalty. In no time, he became the envy of his colleagues and they connived to deal with him. Musa woke up one morning to discover a State Security man at his door with an order from the late dictator for his arrest. When he asked to know what he was being arrested for, they replied: "For plotting to overthrow the military government of General Rambo." Musa was slammed into jail and tortured to the limits of human endurance. The plan was to execute him eventually because coup plotting was treasonable felony and punishable by death.

Fortunately for Musa, General Rambo died before the commencement of his trial and the new government, to gain wider acceptability and legitimacy, released all political detainees and prisoners of conscience thrown into the gulag by the late General. By then however, Musa had developed psychological issues from the trauma of the torture and eventually became insane.

Some people will swear that the latter account was the true version of how Musa went mad. The account I choose to believe though, is the one narrated by Dikko's dad to Dikko and me. According to him, Musa was once a hardworking middle-aged carpenter. He was the best around. He had many customers and his business flourished. He was a good family man who loved his wife and his only child, a daughter, dearly. His perfect world was, however, punctured by the bullets of a policeman. According to Dikko's father, Musa's wife and daughter were shot by a policeman when the driver of the bus they were riding in refused to offer the policeman a bribe of twenty Naira. It was said that the policeman, in annoyance, cocked his rifle and fired at the bus. The bullets missed the driver they were meant for and hit Musa's wife and daughter.

Life became meaningless to him after the loss of his wife and daughter. He disappeared from the town for a very long time only to reappear as a madman. Rumours that made the rounds said he started doing drugs to escape the agony of his bereavement and the drug use eventually drove him mad.

My mind snapped back to the mayhem on the streets. The violence was spreading like an uncontrollable harmattan fire, burning bridges of affection and destroying relationships and lives.

"Look, Balat, this is abominable!" Dikko cried out in horror, pointing his finger in the direction he wanted me to turn.

The sight before me was shocking and blood-curdling. Baba Bulus was pouring petrol all over Malam Adamu's compound. He struck a match as soon as he finished and set the building ablaze. Dikko and I were lost for words. Baba Bulus and Malam Adamu had been friends and next-door neighbours for thirty years.

We heard cries from inside. Malam Adamu and his family were trapped inside the building. I felt a wave of emotion rush through my head. And I felt tears course down my face. Who would ever believe that it was the same Malam Adamu that provided money for Baba Bulus when he had eye surgery? Who would ever believe that when Baba Bulus lost his job at the textile factory, it was Malam Adamu that paid his children's school fees until he got another job as a security guard in another textile factory?

Unfortunately for Malam Adamu, his best friend, Baba Bulus, had joined the people who see themselves primarily as belonging to one faith or the other and allow religious fanaticism and extremism to drive them to mindless and destructive acts.

"Oh Lord, please protect Becky, protect Atimas," I prayed silently.

Since the death of our parents six years ago, and with no known relatives around us, Atimas and I had learnt to depend on and protect each other. Our parents' demise had left us buried in sadness until Becky came into our lives. She brought so much joy to Atimas and me. We were both strongly attached to her. Who wouldn't be?

Becky was all a fellow could ever ask for. She was lovely. Hers was the dream-like beauty of a rose: flawless and perfect in all parts.

I felt so rich and warm whenever she was near. The way she would flow into you, as if she melted into your very bones, was something ethereal. Becky made the earth move for me, she put a gleam in my eyes, a lump in my throat and a bounce in my gait. I swear I would do anything for her. Every time I search for words to explain how I feel about her, I discover that no one can really describe the beautiful, exciting, exhilarating feeling that love evokes. I drifted in the music of Becky's heartstrings; she engaged my artistry daily and filled my world with sweet fragrance. She proved to me quite early on that love is the greatest of all soul forces, the abiding passion, the silver link that binds human hearts together and the mystic power that makes the world go round. Becky was a kindred spirit who shared with me, on many levels of understanding, what life really is.

Many people who knew Becky described her as charming, enchanting and romantic. She was a totally different kind of creature. Many of my friends confessed they had never met one like her before.

Wherever she went, she always stood out from the crowd. I enjoyed taking her out for walks and going to the beach with her. The beach was one place that fascinated her, she enjoyed listening to the rumbles of the sea, the splash of the waves as they cascade over one another, the moan of the wind and the rolling in the sand. At the beach, she was always the cynosure of all eyes. Everybody wanted to play with her, be with her, talk with her, and run with her. Children found her irresistible; teenagers found her adorable; adults wished they had someone like her. Becky was like fine weather – in the same way as when a spell of beautiful weather arrived, you just couldn't help but be delighted when she was around. She was an embodiment of all that was good. Her love was life-giving, it was an expansive, nourishing energy that knew no limits.

She brought out the best in me, a nobility of character. At the touch of her love, I became a poet. I wrote poems for her, love poems that she didn't understand, but she would sit down and listen to them when I read them out. The sparkle in her eyes showed she was just content being with me, listening to my voice, and sharing that intimate moment. Oh, how I wished that dad and mum were alive. They would have loved Becky;

mum in particular would have taken to her. Mum was an incurable romantic while dad wasn't exactly one; however, he was tender-hearted.

My parents loved each other dearly. Unfortunately, death snatched them away in the prime of their lives. It was an untimely death which could have been avoided if only we had had good roads and good healthcare facilities in our country. They were involved in a ghastly motor accident along the Abuja-Kaduna Expressway. It took hours for men of the Road Safety Corps to reach the scene of the accident. And it took them an age to take them to the hospital. Both of them had sustained serious head injuries and lost several pints of blood. When they eventually got to the hospital, they met another shocker, the doctors were on strike over what they considered poor remuneration. None of the doctors was willing to attend to my parents. All appeals to the few of them who were there fell on deaf ears. After hours of fighting to stay alive, my mum and dad gave up the ghost. The Hippocratic Oath was murdered on the altar of inhumanity.

"Balat, Balat, we can move now," Dikko

whispered in my ear, jolting me out of my reverie. The violence had ceased. The messengers of death had taken their merchandise elsewhere to hawk. Dikko and I got up and began what perhaps I may call the longest walk to my house.

When I got home, I wasn't prepared for what I saw. My Becky was lying in a pool of blood which still gushed from a wound in her side. She had suffered a terrible injury. I got down on my knees beside Atimas, who was already in tears. Apparently, she had struggled back home to us. Pain shot up in my brain and rang there like the bell of St Paul's Cathedral. Who could have done this to her? Tell me, who could have done this to Becky? Becky, who was indifferent to religion? Who could have done this great injury to a dog, whose friendship did not pursue selfish advantages, who showed no aggression and was totally trusting?

These questions still beg for answers. As I look back, the bursts of fury, fire and deaths of innocent people and of my beloved dog Becky, are all the more regrettable because so clearly it could all have been avoided.

THORN FROM A ROSE

Dawn came crisp and cold with the treacherous gusts of harmattan wind moaning outside. I was embraced by the cold wind that stabbed through my duvet as I tossed and turned.

Throughout the night, I couldn't sleep a wink because of a letter written by the one who could rightly be described as my power, my pleasure and now my pain. Once again, my eyes fell on the letter. From the content grew the face of the disturber of my dreams; suddenly, she became visible to me.

Before she came into my life like a flood (I swear she drowned my beliefs and replaced them with hers) my existence had been running as smoothly as a dual carriageway. And now she wanted to walk out of my life like that, what wickedness! Tell me, is it a crime to love? What the heck? After all, her reasons for breaking our relationship are flimsy, aren't they? Does the number of moons and seasons seen by the eyes determine whether this love can be?

I used to think the possession of grey hairs was a prerequisite for love. People used to say the older a man becomes the more appealing he is to ladies. But, sincerely, how can age difference be a determinant factor in the growth of true love? If anybody should complain, I should be the one. I could easily have had my pick of any young beauty. Despite my grey hairs, I wasn't bad looking. That I know for sure. A number of ladies told me that I had Denzel Washington's looks and, at my age, I have an athlete's body. One even went further to say that my clothes fit me like a second skin and that my tall, slim features belong on the pages of GQ.

But you know how it is, love is a thunderbolt. Rather, it is a prison: only the object of your love can free you.

I can't run away from the truth. I know that I'm trying to do that. Yes, I know when I see the backside of someone running away from the truth.

Okay! I'll tell you the truth, the whole truth and nothing but the truth. I am enslaved by passion. I, who have survived imprisonment for taking a radical stand against the powers that be, cannot survive this imprisonment. I have become:

> A prisoner to fancies
> In her court I wait
> Longing to be condemned
> To sessions of love songs...
> Decree now! Fair one
> I would I'm guillotined
> Than live in a dungeon
> Of wants, deprived even of the love
> Of one so fair.

And my dear, she is fair, fair as the rose that blooms in May. I must confess, she's a superior being that I must own, a higher class of animal, an angel, an elegant testimony to womanhood.

Her features could not have been more exquisite if they had been carved by a sculptor. Her beauty glows, full of colour, bright as the afternoon sun in Lagos.

Anytime I look into her eyes, fringed with their long lashes, I get so weak in my knees; they are like diamond orbs pitched against a dark night. Her skin is dark and smooth as if perfectly chiselled from dark marble; her voice is a delight to ears. The first time I heard her speak, I was enthralled. When she talks, she polishes her words with the skill of a diamond cutter, revealing facet upon facet of her intellectual refinement.

"I agree with Thomas Hardy that romance should grow up in the interstices of a mass of hard, prosaic reality," she once told me.

I swallowed every word from her mouth. As far as I was concerned, they were life-saving pills. My addiction grew with every dosage. So, you can see why I can't live without her. The thought of evenings deprived of her hit me like ice-cold water gulped down on an empty stomach.

And to think that it was because of her that I broke up with my girlfriend, Betty. I had been seeing Betty for about a year then. I wasn't in love with her but I liked her a great deal. Between you and me, Betty was crazy about me. I remember how shattered she was the day that I told her we had to stop seeing each other. She came to visit me and we were seated by the swimming pool in my house.

"Oh Dafe, please don't go away from me," she said in a tearful voice. "I love you and that is all that matters."

"I know, Betty, but I'm sorry, I have to go. I am in love with somebody else."

She sank down on the floor and started crying. Tears were pouring down her cheeks like rivulets of rain running down the windowpanes of an empty mansion.

The evening breeze skipped across the swimming pool, then paused to run cold fingers through her long, black hair.

I stared at the sky as I waited for her to calm down. The blue sky and the cool Kaduna breeze gave a deceptive look of peace and quiet to the scene. I felt sorry for her but there was really nothing I could do for her. My heart belonged to another woman.

Betty left my house in a distraught state. Just as soon as she left, my best friend, Mike, walked in. He sat his well-built frame on the chair Betty had just vacated. He is of medium height and has dark, curly hair and a complexion like the colour of brown leather. He has a baby face so it is difficult most times for people to tell his age.

"Dafe, what's wrong with Betty? I saw her leaving some minutes ago. She was looking sad."

"I broke up with her, Mike."

"You broke up with her!" Mike was flabbergasted. "Come on man, how could you have done such a thing? Betty really loved you. And please don't tell me you broke up with her because of the so-called love of your life?" he exclaimed.

"Please don't talk about her that way. I've told you so many times that I'm not in love with Betty. Now that I've found somebody I love, I won't allow her to come between us, okay?" I retorted.

But Mike was not ready to rest his case. He told me that she wasn't cut out for me, and she would leave me in no time. How prophetic he was.

She really can't leave like that. I must not let her go. I've been trained not to run away from battle. My years with the military have prepared me for this. I decided I would go to her house, look straight into her eyes and vent my feelings. I swore I would tell her how much I loved her. 'Listen,' I would say, 'If an assassin tried to kill you, I would stop the bullet with my heart.'

'Listen,' I would say, 'I would walk a thousand miles to reach you. I would dig all the gold in South Africa to build a mansion for you.' My mind was made up. I must tell her all these things with that kind of 'frightening persistence' that could raise the titanic.

As I got up from my bed, I heard a knock on my door.

"Yes? Come in."

My mother walked in. As usual a smile was planted on her pretty face and she, the worm eating my thoughts, the moon of my delight walked in in tow.

"Your English teacher is here, Dafe, she has come to bid you goodbye," my mother said.

My heart did a double somersault. All the

words I vowed to tell her died on my lips. My courage fled from me the way Joseph fled from Potiphar's wife.

Miss Sola Ojo, my private English Language and Literature in English teacher stretched out her hands for a handshake. I was scared to take her hand. I knew that just a touch would betray my emotions. An awkward silence fell over the room.

"Come on, Dafe, shake hands with your teacher," my mother said, breaking the silence.

I did, she bade me goodbye and walked out of the room, out of my life. After she left with my mother, I picked up her letter.

I squeezed the letter into a ball and threw it out of the window. Who would believe I had known her for only forty days? Today actually makes it exactly forty days since she was hired by my parents to teach me English Language and Literature in English. Well, I guess she had to go. Miss Sola is twenty-five years old, and I'm only fourteen. She's got her whole life ahead and the same goes for me, too. But I must say, she was my first true love and I know there is still time to fall in love again.

In two days' time, my third-term holidays will be over and I will go back to school at the Nigerian Military School, Zaria, with the ashes of unrequited love. I guess I have to end my story here, but, lest I forget, the letter Miss Sola wrote was a resignation letter to my parents which I purloined from their room. The content simply informed my parents that she had got a job in a bank and could no longer work as my private teacher. She didn't even know that I loved her, I never told her. I wasn't man enough, and my grey hairs are only four in number. My father said I was lucky, that at my age he already had grey hairs all over his head. Some of my uncles also had grey hairs before they reached fifteen. Need I tell you that the times I was imprisoned were times I revolted against my seniors in school? Anyway, thus ends my story of true albeit unactualized love. Ces't la vie. I shall live to love again. Perhaps Betty will forgive and take me back, but that's a story for another day…

LETTER TO GENERAL RAMBO

It is indeed true, to quote Euripides, that: 'No worse foe than the despot has a state, under whom, first, can be no common laws, but one rules, keeping in his private hands the law.' General Rambo, my country's longest serving despot, not only had the law firmly in his hands, but he was very good at applying unlawful force. He was contemptuous of the wellbeing of the citizenry and of world opinion. Thus, he earned the appellation 'Longest Serving Divine Monster'.

Despite the hideous crimes he perpetrated in office, sycophants crowded around him, beating drums of corruption and ethnic jingoism, and singing praise songs, lousy praise songs, for his heinous and repressive practice in office. Must uniformed thugs be elevated to positions of authority to protect and promote the interests of rabid dictators and vagabonds in power?

I must say, I woke up on the right side of my bed that day. I knew that the day was going to be different. It was the twelfth of August, the day earmarked for launching the Campaign for Justice, a human rights group. The launch was billed to take place at the main auditorium of the country's premier university.

A group of young academics like me were the brains behind the group. 'Enough is enough!' we told ourselves. We must not embrace passivity and mute indifference. General Rambo's thugs, tanks, bayonets and sub-machine guns cannot stifle the voice of reason. Neither will they make us cower under oppression.

I had vowed that I would be an indefatigable fighter for freedom and equality and respect for the rule of law.

I left my house, whistling under my breath, my hands buried in my pockets, and strolled leisurely to the launch venue, which was walking distance from the university's staff quarters. Some metres away from the auditorium, I noticed a crowd gathered around one corner and stern-looking policemen and soldiers in combat gear manning the main entrance to the auditorium. I sighted one of my colleagues and walked up to him to find out what was going on. He told me that an order had been issued to stop the launch.

"Where did the order come from?" I asked.

"From above of course," he answered.

I was livid. How dare he, the Monster, infringe on our fundamental human rights. Wasn't it spelt out in the country's constitution that we have the right to freedom of association?

"Power to the people!" I screamed.

"Yes! That's him, that is the leader of the group," a voice said behind me.

A hand quickly grabbed me. Before I knew what was happening, several other hands held on to me. Within a twinkle of an eye, I was down on the ground. I didn't know that some State Security agents had mingled with the crowd, apparently to fish out the ringleaders of the group. They gave me the usual treatment: blows rained down on me. A baton landed on my forehead. Blood began to gush out from the gash on my head. Pandemonium broke out. The cops shot tear gas into the air to disperse the crowd. I was dragged into a waiting police van. And they drove off at high speed. Their mission was accomplished. I was a prize catch.

They took me straight to the office of the Directorate for Intelligence, where I was handcuffed and shown into a room reserved for 'VIPs' – that is, 'Very Important Prisoners.'

The room was small and windowless. A table and a chair were the only furniture. This was placed in the middle of the room; a small bulb hung from the ceiling. Two corporals stood guard to keep an eye on me. One of them was a well-built, middle-aged man of medium height. He had a round face that sat on his thick, heavy neck. He was dark in complexion and wore a permanent scowl on his face. The other guard was tall. His face had a hard, metallic look. His muscles bulged under his uniform. He looked fierce and menacing. I sat on the only chair in the room. Suddenly, the door was flung open and a very tall man walked in. He was dressed in an army uniform and wore the rank of major. He had the big round eyes of an owl. He was light in complexion and clean-shaven.

The two guards stiffened to attention. "Morn Sir!" they saluted. He nodded his head to acknowledge their salute and walked up to me.

"Sorry, Dr Ifeka, I can see you've not been treated well by my boys," he said in a deep baritone voice. He sat on the edge of the table. "I read your articles in the papers. I must say that you write very well. I wonder why you have chosen to use your pen to fight instead of to support the government of the day?"

I kept mute. If he wanted an answer, I wasn't going to give him one.

"You should work with us," he continued. "How much are you paid in the university? You're a young man. You should enjoy the good things of life. If you join the government press, we would pay you a fabulous salary and in fact we will make you the Editor-in-Chief of The Daily Voice."

I still remained calm. I wanted to tell him he

was wasting his breath. Dangling carrots before me would get him nowhere because I would not sell my conscience to dine with the devil of tyranny.

"Well, Dr Ifeka, I can see that you've decided to play dumb with me. I guess I'll have to leave now. When you're ready to talk, tell the boys to call me."

He stood up and walked to the door. He stopped to talk to one of the guards. After the door was closed behind him, the two guards walked up to me. They began to give me the works. I was flogged mercilessly with koboko. The wound on my head was reopened when one of them hit me with the butt of his gun.

I fell to the ground. No part of my body was spared. Blood was running down my face. Lord! They were beating me savagely like a stubborn thief in a market square. I couldn't stand the pain any longer so I started to sing Fela's Zombie.

Zombie no go go
Unless you tell am to go
Zombie
Zombie no go come

Unless you tell am to come
Zombie
Zombie O, Zombie
Zombie O, Zombie.

That infuriated them. With increased vigour, they dealt blows with their gun butts and lashes with the koboko. A kick landed on my groin. A thousand-and-one bombs of pain exploded in my head. Slowly darkness enveloped me and I lost consciousness.

I don't how long I was stretched out on the floor unconscious. I came to full consciousness when cold water was poured on me. I tried to open my eyes. Only one opened. The right eye was swollen shut. The two guards carried me up and sat me on the chair.

"Ah, Dr Ifeka, I can see you've been given our five-star treatment. Are you ready to talk now?" the Major asked.

I tried to say something but blood spilt out of my mouth.

"Look, Dr Ifeka, don't be stubborn. Just cooperate with us. Several charges have been brought against you. First, you have been charged with the illegal importation of arms into the country with the aim to overthrow the government. And you know, under Decree 24, that that offence is punishable by death.

"Secondly, you and others formed the Campaign for Justice, a guerrilla movement, to plunge the country into war. And you, Dr Ifeka, are the leader of the group. Under Decree 32, promulgated today, backdated to the 2nd of last month, that is an offence that is punishable by death."

He stopped to look at me to see if all he had said sank in.

"If you co-operate with us, all these charges will be dropped and immediately you will regain your freedom."

"To hell with you and your charges!" I managed to say.

"Aha! I can see, Dr Ifeka, that you're not ready to co-operate," he said with a wicked gleam in his eyes.

"Corporal Sunday, bring the lady in." The corporal went out and came back with a woman in handcuffs. She wore a white blouse upon a black skirt. Her hair was tied in a bun. She was dark in complexion and her skin shone like polished mahogany. Instantly I recognized the figure, and stared at her in shock, my mouth agape, and blood draining from my face.

"Imelda, what are you doing here?"

"What is she doing here? For your information, we have brought her here so that you can watch us give her the same five-star treatment we gave you," the Major said.

"No! Don't drag her into this," I cried. All the bitterness I felt rose from my belly and choked me in my throat. Lord! What are these beasts up to? I can't allow them to subject the love of my life to the same torture I went through.

"Ify dear, oh my God! What have they done to you?" She turned to the Major: "What do you want from us?" she asked in a tearful voice.

"Good question. First, I want your boyfriend to write an article for The Daily Voice. In the article, he should extol the virtue of the country's Head of State. Secondly, he should stop all his anti-government activities and join hands with the government to move the country forward.

That is all we demand from him."

I was confused. It was a difficult situation. If I wrote the article, they would take it to the government press and it would be published immediately. People would then conclude that I had capitulated and sold out. Nobody would buy the excuse that I wrote it under duress. But if I didn't comply with their demands my dear Imelda would be tortured or worse. I was torn between love for the struggle and love for my fiancée. Now which of them came first in my heart? General Rambo and his goons were demanding a sacrifice. What should I offer? My reputation and the loss of my freedom, or my fiancée?

I looked at Imelda, and that was a mistake. She looked like a frightened child. No longer like an animal in agony. My heart went out to her but I had made my decision. Damn the consequences, after all, as Shakespeare said in Julius Caesar, "Cowards die many times before their death but the valiant taste of death but once…"

My cuffs were removed. I was handed a piece of paper and a biro. I began to write. The article was an open letter to General Rambo.

LETTER TO GENERAL RAMBO

Your Excellency Sir,

First, I'd like to congratulate you on your successful tenure in office for over sixteen years. As the clock ticks slowly, you are heading for your seventeenth year in office. Some despots did not last this long before the wind of change swept them from the corridors of power. I must say that your decision to single-handedly take on the world is commendable.

Some people believe that only an unoriginal power-drunken midget would embark on such an unprofitable venture. I am willing to give you their names and addresses. Such people should be dealt with ruthlessly. To put these people to shame, you should ensure that victory is certain. From all indications, victory shall be yours since you have won the first battle – the battle to make our country a pariah state in the comity of nations.

Our suspension from the Commonwealth of Nations should not bother you. We are no longer under the Queen. So, we don't want the

Queen and her allies to run our affairs for us.

The execution of Basi, the minority rights leader, was a selective justice of injustice. It was the first of its kind in the world. So, what is all the hoopla about his death? Some unpatriotic citizens alleged that Basi was a pain in your neck and that you have never hidden your dislike for men who would not sell their conscience for a mess of pottage. Your detractors believe that Basi's execution has earned you an unenviable place in history. They say posterity will not forgive you for wasting Basi, one of the best brains to come out of our country.

'Who cares?' I am sure you will say. After all, King Herod did something similar to John the Baptist. Believe me, Sir, these so-called critics are actually seeking ministerial appointments.

Your Excellency, continue to promulgate draconian decrees; the systematic elimination of the opposition should be your agenda this year. It is the only way to convince the masses and the Western world that you are a tough enough soldier to rule the country arbitrarily. Your reputation as a maximum ruler is at stake.

Don't do anything that will spoil it. Don't forget that it took you close to sixteen years to get to where you are today.

I advise you to surround yourself with the likes of Baka Biu, your Minister of Misinformation, and also with Madu Benny, your special adviser on matters of the heart and economic affairs. A king should have jesters in his court to amuse him. Your case is no exception. This is the time that you need your jesters most.

Come to think of it, you have done relatively well in the area of population control. Evidence abounds everywhere to show that the economic crunch imposed upon us by your regime is a better means of controlling the population than the Family Control Programme.

Lastly, Sir, you should see the sanctions imposed on the country as a blessing in disguise. The sanctions will completely annihilate the already limping economy. By all means continue to dance in your exquisite finery, visible only to your true acolytes.

Yours faithfully,
Dr Ifeka Alley.

MONEY! MONEY!! MONEY!!!

Oladele Daniels woke up with a great start when he heard a knock on his door. 'Who could that be?' he wondered. A frown spread over his face. He looked at the clock on the wall and it read 10 a.m. He lifted his tall frame slowly from the bed.

"Yes, who is that?" he asked.

"Good morning, sir. I am a representative of the Lagos Lottery Service," came the reply.

"Lagos Lottery what?" He pulled the bolt from the door and opened it. The man outside the door was tall and slim and wore a smile on his dark, handsome face, revealing perfect dentition. He looked more like a model in a toothpaste advert than a representative of the Lagos Lottery

Service. He wore a well-ironed, and obviously starched, immaculate white shirt over a pair of black chinos trousers. The logo of the Lagos Lottery Service was printed on the breast pocket of his shirt. A black baseball cap was balanced on his small head.

"Are you Mr Oladele Daniels with ticket number LL1456?"

"Yes, I am Oladele Daniels and that's my ticket number. May we go inside and talk?"

Oladele Daniels ushered the official into his dingy room. The official's eyes swept the room in a second. The room was small and had only one tiny window for ventilation. A six-spring bed occupied one corner of the room. Two small black pots and a medium-sized kerosene stove occupied another corner. Two shirts and a pair of blue trousers that had seen better days hung on the nail on the wall.

"So, what can I do for you?"

"Well sir, I am happy to inform you that you are the winner of this year's fifty million Naira Lagos Lottery!" the official announced, bursting with enthusiasm.

Oladele Daniels just stared. Incomprehension was etched on his face. Suddenly, the truth hit him.

"Wait a minute! You mean my ticket was picked as the winning ticket for this year's lottery?" He had to be certain he had heard correctly.

"Yes sir," the official answered, beaming with a smile.

Oladele Daniels was flabbergasted. He jumped up and then hugged the official. The smile on his face was bright enough to light up a dark room. He released the man and began to dance round his room. He moved like a drunk high on gin. But he was not drunk with gin. He was drunk with the wine of happiness. He raised a song…

Ose O Baba
Baba oma se,
Olurun mi
Ose O Baba...

The happiness in his voice was palpable. The official from the lottery service joined him. Their singing attracted other tenants in the compound to the room. When he saw his neighbours, Oladele Daniels stooped singing and dancing to tell them the good news. His joy beamed on them like the sun from behind the clouds.

One of his neighbours raised another song which they all joined in singing…

I have a very big God O
Who is standing by my side,
A very big God O
By my side, by my side.

While the singing and the dancing was going on, the official drew Oladele Daniels to a corner.

"Mr Daniels, lest I forget, we want you to come to our office tomorrow afternoon by 1 p.m. to formally receive the fifty million Naira."

"I will be there by 1 p.m. prompt!"

"I'm afraid I'll have to leave now. So, see you tomorrow."

"We must wash am O!" Sanusi, the local neighbourhood drunk, suddenly shouted.

"Why not?" answered Oladele Daniels. He

asked everybody in the room to follow him to Mama Ebuka's beer parlour situated in front of the compound. What other way to celebrate success than with bottles of chilled lager? Mama Ebuka was more than pleased to extend him credit based on his new status!

At night, Oladele Daniels could not sleep a wink. He thought of a million things he would do with fifty million Naira. His brain was working faster than an IBM computer. First, he would buy a duplex in Victoria Garden City or in Dolphin Estate, or perhaps book a suite at the Sheraton Hotel for one year, or maybe buy a duplex at the Marwa Gardens, or… he was undecided. He was still thinking of where to buy a house and what to buy when sleep finally caught up with him.

The next morning, he quickly had his bath and headed for his place of work. In his pocket was two hundred and twenty Naira; it was all the money he had in the world. He worked in the Lagos Railway Station as a booking clerk. Although he knew his absence from work the previous day would earn him a query from the station manager, he was not bothered in the least. In the breast pocket of his white shirt was his resignation letter. Nobody had ever heard of a millionaire working in a railway station. He stopped at the vendor's stand to see if the newspaper carried the news of the result of the Lagos lottery. It did. It was front-page news in all the papers. 'Railway Clerk Wins Fifty Million Naira!' screamed the headline of the story on the front page of The Post. 'Winner of Fifty Million Lagos Lottery Emerges' declared the front page of The Daily Mirror. 'Clerk Becomes Millionaire' bellowed The EKO Times. He bought The Post and went on his way. He walked on clouds. Fortune had finally visited him at the age of thirty-five. In his wildest imagination, he had never thought he would become a millionaire.

When he got to the station, he was surprised to find that a small party had been organized for him by the station manager. His colleagues planted shouts of celebration in his ears. The manager, a short, plump fellow with thick rolls of fat on his neck, was outside his office waiting for him as usual. He had a cigarette stuck between his lips and was puffing away like a locomotive engine.

"Welcome, my boy!" he said.

Oladele Daniels was taken aback by the warm reception. As if the station manager read his mind, he said jocularly: "Hey come off it, will you? I'm not about to issue a query to a man who is worth fifty million Naira!"

The other workers laughed at the joke. This was the first time the station manager had shared a joke with them.

Oladele Daniels relaxed.

After the party, he bade them goodbye and boarded a taxi to the lottery office situated on the Island. He was now a very rich man. His days of riding in molue and danfo buses were over. Perhaps this was to be his last ride in a taxi, too. His first port of call when the fifty million Naira was paid to him would be to buy the Benz 600 S Class, he thought.

"Oga, we don reach de place and ya money na two hundred Naira," the taxi driver said, jolting him out of his daydream.

"Two hundred Naira!" he exclaimed in shock. 'Hey, take it easy boy,' he told himself. How much was two hundred Naira? It was not even up to a drop of his ocean of newfound wealth. He brought the cash out of his pocket and paid the driver. He quickly alighted and half-walked, half-ran to the gate of the Lagos Lottery Service. The official who brought him the good news the day before was already at the gate.

"Welcome Mr Daniels, come quickly. It's twenty minutes to one already, we haven't got much time."

The official led him through the gate into the premises of the Lottery Service. Canopies and chairs were neatly arranged outside. Some invited guests were already seated. Many people had turned up for the ceremony to catch a glimpse of the lucky railway clerk. News crews from different television stations were already setting up their equipment.

The lottery official and Oladele Daniels entered the office complex. They climbed a flight of stairs before stepping into a small hallway that led to the office of the manager of the Lagos Lottery Service.

The manager, a middle-aged man with towering height, wide and powerful shoulders beneath a black jacket, welcomed Oladele Daniels into his office with a broad smile. He showed him the documents to sign. After he had finished signing them, they all trooped down to the presentation venue.

Oladele Daniels was a little disappointed when a fifty million Naira cheque was presented to him. He had expected cash. Nevertheless, it didn't dampen his joyous mood. A cheque was as good as cash, he remembered. Moreover, the manager of the Lottery Service had assured him that the money would be paid into his account as soon as he presented the cheque to any of the branches of Broad Bank, the official bank of the Lottery Service.

At the end of the ceremony, a tight cordon of policemen guarded Oladele Daniels, to protect him from any criminal in the crowd. Despite the cordon of policemen, he did not want to take chances, so he held on tightly to the cheque. As he was being escorted to a waiting police van, a man from the crowd of onlookers suddenly broke through the police cordon, grabbed the cheque from his hands and took to his heels. "Ole! Ole!"

the people screamed. There was a melee. The policemen, Oladele Daniels, the lottery officials and several others were hot in pursuit. The man was racing away like Ben Johnson. The security men at the gate, seeing what had ensued, locked the gate to prevent the thief from escaping. But there was no stopping him. As soon as he got to the gate, something strange happened. He changed into a big black bird and flew away with the fifty million Naira cheque firmly held in its beak.

"Ole! Ole! Ole! My fifty million Naira is gone O!" Oladele Daniels wailed.

"Your fifty million what?"

The voice of the station manager rolled down on him like thunder from the mountaintop.

Oladele Daniels was instantly aroused from his midday nap. When his head cleared, he saw the station manager standing over him. He quickly got to his feet.

"S-o-o-r-r-y sir," he blurted out.

"Sorry for what? You incompetent worker, you are sleeping again on duty. This time around you won't go scot-free. I'll make sure I suspend you without salary for three months," the manager bawled and stormed off arrogantly.

The other clerks in the office broke out in uncontrollable laughter as soon as the station manager walked out of the door, much to the chagrin of the still befuddled and frustrated Oladele Daniels.

FAMILY MATTERS

Pa Efe had just one ambition, to die and escape the rot in his country. From his worn-out clothes and weather-beaten skin, one could tell that he had not led an easy life. He sat on the old wooden chair. His eyes glinted with pain, poverty and dreams unfulfilled.

"Onome! Onome! Onome!" Pa Efe bellowed. 'Where the hell is this boy?' he wondered.

Pa Efe could not hide the frown on his face. He knew Onome had gone out to hang around with area boys. He did not like this. He did not want his first son, a graduate of business administration, to mingle with street urchins and ne'er-do-wells.

"I must put an end to this," he said under his breath.

Pa Efe would be sixty in July this year. He was a former employee of the Federal Ministry of Works and Housing, where he had worked as a site supervisor. Pa Efe was one the workers who lost their jobs in the recent retrenchment exercise. Pa Efe was embittered by this retrenchment. He had served the ministry for thirty years, and he wondered why he should be given the boot just five years to his retirement.

Pa Efe adjusted his tall, lean frame on the chair. Just then, a figure appeared from a corner. It was Onome.

"Good evening Papa," Onome greeted.

"What's good about the evening…eh? Tell me?" Pa Efe retorted.

Onome was confused. He saw the look on his father's face and sensed trouble.

"Where are you coming from?" Pa Efe asked, finally.

"I went to visit my friends."

"Which friends? Tell me, you stupid, good-for-nothing boy! You call those area boys your friends? Those rouges and street urchins. Look, Onome, if you are not ashamed of your unemployment, I am! I spent a fortune to send you to the university, hoping that when you graduate, you will take care of your younger brothers and sisters. You've spent five years at home now after your graduation and, instead of getting yourself a job, you're busy hobnobbing with rascals. Useless boy, son of his mother."

"Yes, I know. Onome's behaviour will always be linked to me, shameless old man," Mama Onome interjected as she came out of her room, where she had been listening to Pa Efe reprimanding Onome. She was fat and of medium height.

"See who is referring to someone as useless, the case of a pot calling the kettle black! Like father, like son. How long have you been sitting at home, eh? Answer me na, shameless man, since you were retrenched last year, what efforts have you made to secure another job? Even if you're of retirement age, that's not an excuse. I have heard of men who are seventy and still working. You lazy man, always blaming me for every misfortune!" She hissed and went inside.

"Yeye woman!" Pa Efe shouted after her. "Now will you move out of my sight?" he shouted at Onome, who was still standing in front of his father.

Onome hurriedly went into the sparsely furnished sitting room.

Pa Efe brought out his pipe and filled it with tobacco. As he smoked, he vowed silently to deal with Mama Onome someday. 'She must be handled with utmost care though,' he thought. Since he lost his job last year, she had been the family's sole provider.

The next day, Mama Onome called her son, Onome, into her room. She too was worried about Onome's nonchalant attitude towards getting a job. She remembered how, after his National Youth Service, he had combed the streets of Lagos in search of a job.

Onome broke into her thoughts when he came into the room.

"Yes Mama, I heard you calling my name."

"Eh o, my son, indeed I called you, I want you to sit down. I have something important to discuss with you."

Onome sat on the bed.

"Onome! Onome! Onome! How many times did I call you?" she asked.

"Three times, Mama."

"Our people say that one can take a horse to the river but you cannot force it to drink."

"It is true, Mama," Onome agreed.

"You see, my son, we have done our best by sending you to school. We had hoped that when you graduate and start working, you'd be able to help us. I know that jobs are difficult to find these days, but that doesn't mean that you should relent on your efforts. But you have to stop hanging out with those street boys you call your friends. We have given you education; it is up to you to use it to better the lot of your family. Heaven helps those who help themselves. Don't wait for manna to fall down from heaven. Think of what you can do to earn money. I am not saying you should go and steal. There are many graduates who are conductors, bus drivers and cleaners. It is not a must you start from the top. You can start from the bottom and work your way up."

She went on: "I know that with your

qualifications you should be aiming for a white-collar job but, failing this, what will you do? Your father's old Peugeot 504 is there. If you are ready to use it as a taxi, I will lend you money to buy tyres and repair the engine. When your father lost his job, I told him to repair that car and use it for taxi business. He complained that he had no money. I told him that I'll borrow from my club for him to repair the car. He stuck to his guns. He told me that he didn't want my money. I also remember he told me that as an ex-senior supervisor in the Federal Ministry of Works and Housing he couldn't belittle himself by driving a taxi around town.

"You can see we are suffering now; your father does not give me money. I am now the breadwinner of the family. The weight is really on my shoulders. Your younger brother, Edirin, has finished secondary school, he has to go to the university, Uzoezi is there too. I have to pay her fees and buy books for her. Things are not easy my son, so please try and do something to help me out. But I must reiterate that I am not asking you to go and steal. Think about what I've told you. If you make up your mind, don't hesitate to tell me."

"Thank you, Mama, for your advice. I'll think about all you've said." Onome stood up and took his leave.

The Oghales, as Pa Efe's family was known, were a peace-loving family, but ever since Pa Efe lost his job peace had fled from his household.

Pa Efe married late in life; he was thirty-four years old when he married Mama Onome. A year after their wedding, Mama Onome gave birth to Onome. It was that same year, 1970, that the Nigerian Civil War ended. Pa Efe was transferred to Lagos from Port Harcourt in 1971. He had been living in Lagos ever since. He had spent twenty-five years in Lagos city. Pa Efe was blessed with five children; Onome – twenty-five years old, Edirin – twenty years old, Uzoezi – nineteen years old, Edoja – seventeen years old, Eloho – fifteen years old.

Before he lost his job, he was a senior supervisor, grade one in the ministry. Pa Efe had worked hard to get to that position, despite his lack of educational qualification. Pa Efe got to a position hitherto reserved for Secondary School Certificate holders. Pa Efe could only boast of a Standard Six certificate. He started as a labourer in the ministry and moved steadily up the rungs of the ladder. His rise to the position of supervisor spanned thirty years.

He grew up in Ozoro, a town in Isoko Local Government Area in Delta State. He left his village at the age of twenty-five to seek greener pastures in the city. Port Harcourt was his first destination where he secured a job with P.W.D., as the then Public Works Department was called (also known as "Poor man, Work and Die" in local parlance). It is now the Federal Ministry of Works and Housing.

"Papa! Papa!" Edirin shouted from outside. Pa Efe had been sleeping in the sitting room. He woke up with a start. He was furious. 'Edirin must have a good reason for screaming, else I will deal with him severely,' he muttered to himself.

Edirin rushed into the sitting room waving a piece of paper. He saw the look on his father's face and stopped. The excitement on his face died immediately.

"Papa, sorry to disturb you," he said, noticing that he had just woken his father from his nap. "Papa, I have good news for you."

"What is the good news?" Pa Efe asked gruffly.

"I scored two hundred and seventy in the J.A.M.B. exams!" Edirin declared.

"Oh, that is good news," Pa Efe said, now beaming with smiles.

"What school did you choose?"

"Papa, you have forgotten so soon?"

"Don't blame me, my son, I have so many things on my mind."

"University of Lagos," Edirin announced.

"So, what is the cut-off mark for Mechanical Engineering?" Pa Efe asked.

"I don't know, Papa, but I'm sure it will not be more than two hundred and seventy."

"Anyway, I'll go to the university tomorrow to check," said Pa Efe. "That reminds me, I have a cousin there, o yes ... Edafe, that's his name, he is the assistant registrar in charge of admission. I'll talk to him and see if he can assist you in any way."

"Thank you, Papa" Edirin said. He gave the J.A.M.B. result slip to his father.

Pa Efe could not go back to sleep. He sat on the long settee. A smile lit up his face like fluorescent tubes. His sons were not letting him down.

"Why are you smiling?" Mama Onome asked, walking into the sitting room. She dropped the basket she was carrying and sat on the sofa.

"Don't I have a right to smile in my own house?" Pa Efe asked, his eyes suddenly blazing.

"Ah sorry o, landlord, I didn't mean to insult you," Mama Onome answered.

"He handed the result slip to her. She looked at it, incomprehension etched on her face. "What is this?" she asked.

"Your son's results slip," Pa Efe said, looking at her with a mischievous glint in his eyes.

"You know I cannot read and write," she said.

"Oh, I forgot that you never saw the four walls of a classroom."

"Did he pass?" she asked, ignoring Pa Efe's remark.

"Yes, he scored two hundred and seventy.

That should give him a place in the university."

"But, Papa Onome, even if he gains admission, where will the money to sponsor him come from?" she asked.

"Don't worry, woman. God will provide."

"God will provide, that is all you say! When I advised you to save for the rainy day, you turned a deaf ear to my advice, you spent your money on alcohol, women and gambling. Shameless man! I hope you'll send him to school with your teeth," Mama Onome exclaimed.

"Look here woman, I won't be insulted by you. My son will go to school. I don't blame you; you don't value education. I'm not surprised, after all, nobody in your family saw the four walls of a classroom. I am happy Edirin is not as dull as your brothers…"

"Eh, eh, eh" Mama Onome cut in. "Don't insult my brothers yeye fowl, I am not ready to exchange words with you this evening." She got up from the sofa and quickly went into the kitchen.

Mama Onome was not far from the truth when she said Pa Efe did not save for the rainy day. He spent his money on women and alcohol; his romance with lager beer and pools betting was the stuff of legends.

***

Pa Efe was ushered into his cousin's office by the latter's secretary, a dark, tall, beautiful girl with enchanting eyes. He could not take his eyes off the girl. The girl swung her hips provocatively. When Pa Efe entered her boss's office, she closed the door behind him and went back to sit at her desk.

Pa Efe's gaze fell on the man sitting on the big executive chair. The last time he set eyes on his cousin had been ten years ago.

"Welcome brother," the man greeted. "How's your family?" he asked, beaming with smiles.

"They are fine."

"Please sit down."

"Na wa o, long time no see, I can see you've really changed. You've grown fat and your stomach is protruding. I guess it is the evidence of good living," Pa Efe said jokingly.

"Yes brother, it seems like ages since we last saw each other. You know how my job is, I'm always travelling and I've been very busy. What can I offer you?"

"Nothing my brother," Pa Efe said, looking at his cousin.

'He has really changed,' Pa Efe thought, remembering that twenty years ago Edafe was just a young undergraduate at the University of Lagos. 'Look at him today, he's already a big shot. Edafe who was very thin when he was young is now very fat; Edafe is now a big man, education is really good o, it catapults you to the top.'

"Brother, how's Onome?" Edafe asked, breaking into Pa Efe's thoughts.

"Oh, he is fine."

"I guess by now he should have graduated from the university."

"Yes, my brother, he graduated five years ago from the University of Benin, he studied business administration."

"So, what is he doing now?"

"He is unemployed, you know jobs are difficult to find these days."

"How is Edirin?"

"Edirin is fine, he just received his J.A.M.B. result slip. In fact, that is the main reason for my visit."

"What did he score?"

"Two hundred and seventy."

"Two hundred and seventy!" Edafe exclaimed. "Well, that's a good score. What course did he choose?"

"Mechanical Engineering."

"Wait, let me check the cut-off mark for Mechanical Engineering…" He stared at the document for about forty seconds, then looked up with a worried look on his face.

"I'm afraid we have a problem here."

"What is the problem?" Pa Efe asked, anxiously.

"The cut-off mark for Mechanical Engineering is two hundred and seventy-one."

"Two hundred and seventy-one!" Pa Efe exclaimed. "Well, are there ways you can squeeze Edirin in, maybe help him to get in through the second batch?"

"I'm afraid, brother, there's nothing I can do, it's not possible."

"But my brother, he just fell short by one mark, his score should give him a place in the second batch..."

"Brother, you know how rigid the admission policy of this school is. And, as you already know, so many candidates applied for admission into the Engineering Faculty. The competition is stiff. Over three hundred candidates scored above two hundred and seventy-one. The university is going to take only two hundred candidates into the Engineering Faculty."

"Can he change to another department, maybe to Physics?" Pa Efe pleaded.

"Well, I'll see what I can do about it, the cut-off mark is two hundred and sixty-nine. So, I guess he'll be accepted in that department."

"That'll be great. Thanks for your help," Pa Efe said rising from his seat to shake hands with Edafe. They bade each other goodbye.

Immediately after Pa Efe left, a man walked into Edafe's office. He was dressed in a white flowing gown. He exuded affluence.

"Ah Chief, welcome sir, please sit down."

Chief Layi Thomas was a rich businessman, chairman of DAV Merchant Bank.

"Chief, what do I offer you?"

"Nothing, thanks anyway."

Chief Layi Thomas cleared his throat and began to speak.

"My son's J.A.M.B. result is out, he scored two hundred. I don't know if you'll be able to help him gain admission into the University of Lagos?"

"Ah, ah Chief, you shouldn't have bothered coming. You mean you left your office because of Dele's admission? You shouldn't have done that. I know you are a very busy man, haba Chief? At least you could have sent your driver or called me on the phone. By the way, which course did he choose?"

"Mechanical Engineering," Chief Layi Thomas answered.

"That's no problem, I assure you he'll be admitted. The cut-off mark is two hundred and seventy-one, but I'll do my best possible to squeeze him in," Edafe said.

"Thank you, Mr Admissions, here is a gift for Madam and the children." Chief Layi Thomas handed a brown envelope containing twenty thousand Naira to Edafe.

"I better be on my way."

The Chief left, promising to call back some other time.

***

"Good afternoon," Pa Wale greeted, entering the compound. As usual, Pa Efe sat on his favourite chair on the veranda. Pa Wale was sixty-four years old; he was tall and had a complexion the colour of leather. His eyes were dark brown, the whites not clear and they were also dulled by poverty.

"Hello Wale, welcome to my humble abode. Edirin! Edirin!"

"Yes, Papa."

"Bring a chair for Pa Wale."

Pa Wale was Pa Efe's best friend. They had been friends since their days in the ministry. Like Pa Efe, Pa Wale lost his job in the shake-up.

"Old boy, what is happening?" Pa Wale asked.

"Nothing o, just sitting down as usual praying that manna should fall from heaven," Pa Efe answered.

"I learnt you went to the university yesterday.

I saw Eridin and he told me you went there to pursue his admission. So how was your trip?"

"Fine. I met my cousin, you remember Mr Edafe, the Assistant Registrar in charge of Admissions. He promised to help. I hope that something good happens..."

"You don't sound optimistic," Pa Wale remarked.

"Ah, don't blame me, my friend, for sounding pessimistic. Who would not be pessimistic? Imagine a boy score two hundred and seventy, and he is denied admission to study Mechanical Engineering?"

Pa Efe went on to narrate what transpired between him and his cousin.

"Oh, I see," Pa Wale said after Pa Efe finished his narration.

"The most annoying aspect of it all is, candidates whose parents are wealthy and who did not score up to two hundred and seventy will gain admission. I learnt from a reliable source that if you can pay fifty thousand Naira to the officials in J.A.M.B. your ward will be given admission letter to any university of his choice."

"Efe, that is no news, there is an admission racket in J.A.M.B. A Vice Chancellor in one of our universities openly said that admission into his school is for sale. You see, our education sector is in shambles. People who are not university material now gain admission into the university through the back door. It is little wonder that secret cults in our citadels of learning are on the rise daily. What do you expect from people who are not university material?" Pa Wale said, wiping sweat from his brow.

"Corruption has eaten deep into the fabric of our society. Our leaders have institutionalized corruption in Nigeria. Education is no longer for the poor. W.A.E.C. charges exorbitant fees for Senior Secondary School examination. Now, tell me, do you expect these kids to pay two thousand Naira and not do anything within their power to pass the examinations? Some of these students go out of their way to buy question papers before the examination. Instead of studying, they think of various ways to cheat during the examinations."

"Do you blame the kids?"

"Not in the least! We, the older generation, have set bad examples. These children believe that since we, the elders, cheat during elections and embezzle funds, what stops them from looking for shortcuts towards achieving success?"

"I blame our leaders for all our woes," Pa Efe lamented.

"Efe, we are all guilty, the leaders and followers are guilty. We should search our conscience and look for what we hid from ourselves."

"Abeg Wale, let's forget Nigeria and think of something better to discuss. Only God can save this country," Pa Efe said. "Edirin! Edirin! Bring the draughts outside, and don't forget to bring a stool."

"Efe, I am going to beat you silly today."

"Look who's talking, my middle name is draughts and you know I am the undisputed champion in the game of draughts …"

"Stop boasting, after the game we will know who is who," Pa Wale said.

***

Dr Bandele Badmus's imposing mansion was the outstanding house on the street. It was painted white. The mansion would make Italian architects green with envy. Onome spotted the house from a distance and his heart began to thump with excitement. Although he was a little nervous, he had made up his mind to visit Tinuke. He had read somewhere that it was risky not to take a risk. To him, this was a risk worth taking. He braced himself as he approached the house.

Tinuke was the only child of Dr Bandele Badmus, a multi-millionaire and medical practitioner with a big hospital on Lagos Island.

Onome met Tinuke at a party.

They had got to know each other very well and he promised to check on her.

At twenty-two, Tinuke was already a ravishing beauty, tall and built like a gazelle, with a lovely face, shapely legs and a complexion like polished mahogany. Her teeth were as white as snow, while her hazel eyes were simply magical. She had graduated from the University of Lagos in business administration.

Onome was enchanted the very first time he set eyes on her; her bewitching beauty made her irresistible.

Onome rang the bell. He waited for some minutes before he heard footsteps. He was conscious of being watched from inside. The security guards must been observing him from the closed-circuit TV. The gate was opened by one of the guards, a northerner.

"Yes? Na who you dey look for?" the guard asked. He sized Onome up with his eyes.

"Tinuke," Onome answered.

"Wetin be your name," he barked?

"Onome."

"Madam get am for appointment with you?" he asked in bad pidgin English.

"Yes," Onome lied. Tinuke was not expecting him. His visit was intended to surprise her.

The guard picked up the phone in the guards' booth and called the main house. He spoke for about one minute then dropped the receiver.

"You fit go inside, madam dey wait for you."

"Thank you."

The uniformed steward ushered him into a tastefully furnished living room. Onome was dazzled by the elegance and beauty of the room. The furniture was exquisite. The Persian rug under his feet was soft. Onome liked the colour of the rug. It was blood red. He glanced around the room appreciatively. He could see beautiful paintings on the wall. It was obvious that the artwork was expensive. The opulence was mesmerizing. The affluence of the owner of the house was richly displayed in this room.

"Hi?" a sweet voice greeted.

He looked up and saw Tinuke smiling at him. He had not heard her come in. She wore a beautiful white FUBU T-shirt over a pair of black DKNY jeans.

"Hello," he answered.

"What a surprise visit, I must say. Please sit down. What can I offer you?"

"Malt, please."

She rang for the servant, who came in immediately as if he had been expecting the call.

"Please, Akan, bring two bottles of malt drink."

The servant quickly went in and came back in no time with the drinks.

Tinuke sat on a chair across from him. They chatted for some time about this and that. Tinuke told Onome about her school days whole Onome regaled her with an account of his.

"Well, Onome, what are your plans for now?" she asked, after she learnt of his prolonged unemployment.

"Well, Tinu, I really don't have any plans for now, I'm still keeping my fingers crossed. I've written several applications. I'm sure one of these days something will come up."

"What about your dad, can't he help you in any way?" she asked.

Onome told her about his dad's situation. He was surprised he could open up to a girl he'd just met. Tinuke was the kind of girl you couldn't lie to because you could easily trust her, like the sinner that goes to church to confess his sins to the priest and is assured that his confession will not make the priest dislike or judge him. Onome did not hide anything from her. Tinuke was so easy to talk to; you felt you could tell her anything and everything.

Moreover, Onome had resolved that he would never lie to any girl again. An incident that occurred in the past was still fresh in his memory. He remembered Ann, a petite girl; she had been his course-mate in school.

Ann was the kind of girl who went out with guys from well-to-do homes. Onome wanted her badly. He vowed to get Ann by hook or by crook. When he eventually got the chance to woo her, he lied that his father was rich. Onome told her that he travelled to London and New York frequently. Ann fell for his lies and went out with him. Onome was able to convince her with his lies because he had some money to throw around at the time. He wore good clothes, so it was difficult for Ann to suspect he wasn't telling the truth.

During the holidays, Ann decided to pay Onome a surprise visit. Onome had concealed his address from her. In fact, when she asked for his address, he told her not to bother because he would be travelling to London and wouldn't be back till the holidays were over.

Ann was determined to check on him. She wanted to meet Onome's family at all costs as she was hoping that their relationship would be cemented during the holidays. She got Onome's address from one of his friends, who was unaware of Onome's strategy.

Ann was at first shocked to find out that Onome lived in Okokomaiko, a suburb along Badagry Expressway in Lagos. She quickly put her doubts behind her. She told herself that perhaps Onome's dad was one of those millionaires who did not want to live in Victoria Island or Ikoyi.

She boarded a bus from Mile 2 to Okokomaiko. When she got to her destination she alighted, and with the help of a boy she was able to trace Onome's house. When she got to the house, she was once again shocked. The house she beheld was an unpainted face-me-I-face-you compound. She asked the boy who took her there if he was sure the house was No 4 Hassan Street, and the boy gave an affirmative nod.

She went in and met an elderly woman sitting on the veranda.

"Good afternoon ma."

"Good afternoon my daughter."

"Abeg ma, I dey look for one boy wey dem

dey call Onome," she said in pidgin English.

"Onome?"

"Yes ma, im be student for University of Benin."

"Na my pikin be that, anything? Any wahala?"

"I be im schoolmate."

"Oh o, welcome my daughter, make we go inside."

She was shown into the sitting room. The furniture in the sitting room had seen better days. The rug on the floor was threadbare. A black-and-white TV stood on a table in a corner of the room.

"My daughter, wait make I go call am, he dey backyard dey wash cloth." She left her alone and went out to call Onome.

Ann heard voices from the bedroom. Suddenly a child cried out: "Give me my groundnut!" Another voice answered: "Which groundnut? Di one wey you take drink garri no reach you?"

A boy ran out of the room clutching a bowl of garri soaked in water.

"Yes, una don start again abi?" Mama Onome asked the child. "I no blame una because una see garri das why una dey misbehave, some people dey wey no dey see this kind food chop..."

"Mama na Edirin dey look for my trouble, e take my groundnut, na im I carry the plate of garri run," the child who was reprimanded a minute before answered.

The conversation between mother and son did not escape Ann's sharp ears. She was numbed with shock. So Onome had been lying all along?

Onome walked in, wondering who had come to see him. He was astonished to see Ann. He prayed that the ground would open up and swallow him.

"What a..r..e you do..ing here?" he managed to stutter.

"I should be asking you that question," Ann replied. She went on: "I thought you ought to be in London by now? Millionaire's son, what happened to your father's riches, wretched soul?" She looked at Onome disdainfully. "Anyway, I don't think I want to stay in these squalid surroundings any minute longer."

She stood up and took her leave. Onome did not bother to call her back. He knew that it was over between them, and he was certain that his reputation in school was at stake.

His encounter with Ann taught him a major lesson.

He spent some time with Tinuke before taking his leave. He promised to check on her again.

***

No 4 Hassan Street was like any other compound in the Okokomaiko area. The tenants were low-income earners. The building was still unpainted years after completion. Despite the filth in the compound, the landlord, Alhaji Kareem Abdul, charged exorbitant rents. Quarrels among the tenants were frequent. To some tenants, a day without quarrelling with their neighbours was incomplete.

The compound was big. It had twenty-four rooms and over two hundred people lived in the place. These people shared two bathrooms, two toilets and one kitchen. The condition of the place would shock sanitary inspectors. To go to work early, you had to wake up as early as 3am to have your bath. If you woke up later, you would be stuck in a long queue, because about ninety percent of the tenants were up at that time and heading for the bathroom too.

Every year the population of the compound increased. A man with seven children would still want to have another child. The average number of children per family in the compound was nine. The bachelors in the compound were very few. Baba Bomboy, an old tenant in the compound, held the record of 'the man with the highest number of children in Hassan Street'. He had twelve children from one woman. He often boasted that "children are riches, they bring wealth". It was hard to believe him when you considered that, despite the number of children he had, he was still poor and found it difficult to feed them. Baba Bomboy and his family lived in abject poverty. Mama Bomboy, his wife, opined that family planning was not part of our culture and she would have no part of it.

Ironically, she would be the first to lament that, had Baba Bomboy not ignored family planning, they would not have found it difficult to feed the children. It was a big burden to supply the needs of the family and it was really difficult to make ends meet.

Onome woke up with a start. "It's 7am already," he muttered to himself. He was woken up by the shouts of two women. He remembered his date with Tinuke and quickly got up from his bed. "Oh, not again, he murmured to himself. These women and their quarrels." He could hear the voices clearly. He picked out Mama Bomboy's voice...

"Yeye woman, Asewo, you think say I no know?"

"Na so you go dey eye people husband, look make I tell you; Papa Bomboy no get time for fatty bumbum like you, you hear me so?" Mama Bomboy shouted.

"I don suffer, see me see trouble, Mama Bomboy wetin I get to do with your husband? I know get my own husband? Tell me, who go eye man wey im eyes be, like frog and im head big like Falomo bridge! Na now I know say you dey jealous me, na true Mama Caro talk, yes, na true, you dey really jealous me because I don dey make money from the okro and tomatoes business wey I just start. I don notice am since I start de business, if I greet you, you go troway face as if you no see me and use nose answer me, jealousy go kill you and that your husband with one kain eye to pick quarrel with me oloshi," Mama Chinwe retorted, her eyes blazing. She was ready to pounce on Mama Bomboy.

The other tenants pretended not to notice the quarrel. Mama Bomboy and Mama Chinwe were always at loggerheads. The other tenants vowed that they would never wade into their affairs again. But they were forced to break their vow when the two women started fighting. The other tenants knew that if the situation got out of hand the police would be invited and everybody would be quizzed and taken to the police station, either to be detained or for further interrogation and bribes would have to paid.

"She don bite me o!" Mama Chinwe cried out. "The witch don bite me o, I know go gree, make una no divide us o, we go kill each other today."

The tenants held her tightly; she struggled to free herself from their grip. She was wailing. She pleaded with them to let her go and teach Mama Bomboy a bitter lesson. Mama Chinwe felt cheated. From the size of both women, it was obvious that Mama Chinwe would have the upper hand in any fight between them. She was built like a truck, very big and muscular, while Mama Bomboy was thin as a rake.

Some of the tenants succeeded in calming her down. She was taken to the backyard.

Some women in the compound dragged Mama Bomboy to the frontage. She was relieved that the fight was over, at least temporarily. She knew that if the fight had lasted longer, Mama Chinwe would have killed her. She thanked her "chi" for saving her from the clutches of Mama Chinwe. Who would not be scared of a woman that fights like Lennox Lewis? So don't blame or call Mama Bomboy a lazy woman.

***

Onome alighted from the taxi and paid his fare.

His wristwatch told him that he was right in time. He walked up to Tinuke's gate. He rang the doorbell and waited patiently for the guard to open the gate; Onome was shown inside. He entered the living room; an elderly man was sitting on the long settee, his head buried in a newspaper.

"Good afternoon sir," Onome greeted.

The man looked up. "Good afternoon, you must be Onome. Tinuke is expecting you, please sit..."

"Onome! So you're here?" Tinuke said, entering the living room. A smile was planted on her face. "I saw you come in." She sat down near her father. "Dad, meet my friend Onome."

"How do you do? Sit down." Onome sat down. "I've heard so much about you."

Tinuke rushed back to her room to pick up her handbag. She came back in no time.

"Dad, I'm going out with Onome," she said, kissing her daddy goodbye.

Tinuke did not want him to start interrogating Onome.

Onome's relationship with Tinuke blossomed.

They loved each other dearly. They were caught up in the whirlwind of romance. It wasn't long before Tinuke's parents got to know about the relationship.

Dr and Mrs Bandele Badmus were not happy with this development. They learnt from Tinuke that Onome was unemployed. Mrs Badmus could not fathom how on earth her only daughter could date an unemployed graduate. The fact that Tinuke was seriously involved with him gave her no joy. She was also irked by the fact that Onome was not from a well-to-do family. She gleaned this information from her daughter.

Dr Badmus and his wife resolved to have a heart-to-heart with their daughter. They wanted her to go out with someone from their class and not a nobody. Mrs Badmus had laid out plans for a grand wedding for her daughter. She wondered why Tinuke should choose a poor man's son.

Her mind wandered to Ade, a young man from a rich home who was head-over-heels in love with Tinuke. He wanted her hand in marriage badly. Ade was from a very rich family. His dad was the owner of the largest pharmaceutical company in

Nigeria. Ade, a lawyer, was the perfect match for Tinuke. Her mother did her very best to make Tinuke accept Ade, but her daughter rebuffed his advances.

Mrs Badmus doted on Tinuke, of course. As an only child, she had her mother's complete attention. Tinuke was her mother's joy, her jewel of inestimable value, and Mrs Badmus believed that parents had the right to choose partners for their children. Tinuke did not agree with her mother, and thought she was interfering in her personal life.

When Tinuke came home in the evening her parents informed her that they would like to have a discussion with her.

She joined them in the living room. She kissed her parents both on their cheeks and sat down on the settee with them. She was sandwiched between them.

Her father cleared his throat and began: "Tinuke, you know how much I love you. When you were born, I vowed that you were going to get the best education and that the man you would marry would be a nice, responsible young man from a respectable family." He stopped talking to look Tinuke in the eye, then continued: "Tinuke, I must say categorically, without mincing words, that your mother and I are not happy with you. The reason for our sadness is not difficult to see. Your relationship with that boy called Onome is giving us heartache. We believe that he is not good enough for you. It is apparent that your relationship with him has no future. I do not want my own child to have an affair with an irresponsible unemployed graduate..."

"Dad!" Tinuke cried out. "I would not have you insult Onome in my presence."

"Will you shut up!" her father commanded. "You have the audacity to tell me not to insult your boyfriend? You must be crazy. You must stop seeing that poverty-stricken fellow!" he shouted.

Tinuke flinched. She looked at her mother, wanting her to intervene.

Her mother did intervene. She did not like the way her husband was handling the matter. His attitude would only push Tinuke further towards Onome.

"Tinuke, my daughter."

"Yes mum."

"My daughter, you have to be realistic, you are from a wealthy family, you were born with a silver spoon in your mouth and grew up in riches. It is imperative that you marry someone from a rich home, who'll provide all you know and give you the comfort you're used to. The truth is you'll not survive if you marry someone who cannot give you the comfort you're used to. After two years you'll be frustrated..."

"But mum, I really love Onome. I don't believe money has got anything to do with love. I love him with all my heart, love is ..."

"Look, Tinuke, you have to face facts. Love is no longer blind in Nigeria. Love had got eyes, four eyes, two in front and two behind. You can love a man with all your heart if he supplies all your needs. Nowadays, when a woman says a man is caring and loving, it means that the man caters for most of her needs. And when a woman says a man is uncaring, rest assured that the man is either poor, flat broke or has stopped catering for her. So, my dearest daughter, there is more to love than meets the eyes. You have a young man from a respectable home dying to have your hand in marriage. Don't waste your time running after Onome or whatever you call him, Ade is the right man for you. He loves you and wants you badly, and your father and I like him."

"Mum, I don't love Ade, Onome is the only man I love. If you and dad are worried about his unemployment, then give him a job. Dad, at least you should be able to find a place for him in one of your companies. The fact that he is unemployed and from a poor home is no fault of his. You know jobs are not easy to come by these days. Our economy is bad. So many graduates are unemployed. Onome is just a victim of the system. He is among the unfortunate majority. These people have done everything within their means to get jobs, all to no avail. They continue to hope against hope that someday they'll pick up jobs. I'm ready to wait for Onome and nothing is going to stop me from loving him."

Her parents were numb with shock.

"I must reiterate that I don't want to see you with that wretched young man again. The day I see that thing in my house again, I will deal with him!" her father retorted.

Tinuke stormed out of the living room and ran upstairs crying.

***

The next day, Tinuke met Onome at their favourite hang out in FestacTown, Tantalizers.

"Tinuke, what are we going to do?" Onome asked after Tinuke finished narrating what had transpired at home.

"I don't know," she answered.

Onome was lost in thought. He had to do something. Things were getting out of hand. His parents, his dad in particular, was always nagging him. His continued stay at home was becoming intolerable.

"What kind of country is this?" he asked no one in particular. "A country where jobs are difficult to find is no country," Onome thought. 'The youths do not have a future in this country. So many people are living from hand to mouth. Some years ago, it was uncommon to hear of unemployed graduates taking to armed robbery, but nowadays it is no longer news. Most robbers these days are graduates! Nigerians including Ph.D. graduates are now fleeing the country in droves in search of greener pastures. Many Nigerian graduates sweep the streets in European cities like London, Berlin, Paris, Amsterdam, to mention but a few. You can find some of them in the United States of America. Nowadays it pays to be a footballer rather than waste precious time getting educated. The government even attaches more importance to football than education, or tell me how can one explain a situation where the government doles out millions to footballers and cannot pay the salaries of teachers? The university calendar has been disrupted several times due to the incessant strikes by the University staff unions. Their bone of contention has always been poor wages. Do you blame them? I don't. Their wages are a huge joke…'

Onome was angry, angry with the leaders of Nigeria, his country past and present, the politicians and the military for pushing the country to the edge of the precipice. His beloved country was in the throes of economic ruin. These so-called leaders were men who would sell their mothers to the devil for money. Instead of improving the lot of the masses, they had subjected them to untold hardship. Embezzling funds from the nation's treasury was their favourite pastime. To make matters worse, these executive thieves unashamedly flaunted their ill-gotten wealth. Corruption had been institutionalized in the country. To be corrupt was one of the prerequisites to hold public office. In fact, corruption was no longer a vice but a virtue in Nigeria. Onome could not help but wonder why the country should continue to suffer from the depravities of corrupt rulers. He was however, optimistic that someday things would get better. He heaved a long-suffering sigh.

"Onome, you look worried. What are you thinking about?" Tinuke asked, disturbing his train of thought.

"Nothing," he lied.

"Don't give me that, you had a worried look on your face a moment ago. Look, Onome, I know you're troubled," Tinuke said, taking Onome's hand. "My dearest Onome, I want you to rest assured that I'll always love you. Things shall be all right. We can cross the hurdles together. No matter the obstacles on our way, we shall always triumph. My parents cannot stop me from loving you. You are everything to me. My love for you is deeper than the deepest ocean."

Onome squeezed her hands: "Tinu, my love for you is endless."

They were silent for some minutes, then suddenly a smile lit up Tinuke's face. "Hey, I've got a brilliant idea, I've been thinking about it for some time. Have you ever thought of leaving this country?"

"Yes, but I always put the thought behind me. Why did you ask? What have you got up your sleeves?"

"I have two hundred and sixty thousand Naira in my account, I could give you the money."

"No, Tinuke, I don't want you to give me your money. What would your dad say when he finds out that you've emptied your account…?"

"Nonsense, it is my account, I can withdraw money from it anytime I want to," she retorted.

"Now let's start planning. You need about three hundred thousand Naira to travel to London. You already have two hundred and sixty thousand. Let's work it out how are we going to raise the remaining forty thousand."

Onome was deeply touched by her kind gesture. He knew very well that if he refused the offer she would be offended. Come to think of it, he had nothing to lose. Moreover, he had no other option. It was an offer he couldn't refuse. He remembered one of his father's proverbs; "If you put sugar in the mouth of a child, he will never spit it out."

***

"Mama Onome! Mama Onome!" Pa Efe shouted.

"What is it, Pa Efe?" Mama Onome said, going outside to meet Pa Efe. "Pa Onome, it's too early to start shouting. Do you want to wake our neighbours?"

"My car! My car! It is missing, my car has been stolen, oh I'm finished, my enemies want me to die wretched!" Pa Efe wailed.

Mama Onome was shocked to discover the 504 was missing from the spot where it had been parked in the compound. Someone had stolen the car. Who could have done this? she asked herself. The other tenants in the house ran out, alarmed by Pa Efe's yelling.

"Pa Efe calm down, you will find the car," one of them said.

"Let's report the theft to the police," another suggested.

They all agreed that it was the best thing to do.

Pa Efe and some tenants trooped down to the police station, which was not far from their compound. Pa Efe reported the theft of his car, and the police promised to look into the matter. They asked Pa Efe to write a statement. He did and was told to go home. Pa Efe was certain that if he didn't offer a bribe to the police officers in charge of his case, nothing would come out of their investigation. Corruption had eaten deep into the Nigerian Police Force. The bad eggs in the force outnumbered the good ones. "Egunje has spoilt Lagos," he muttered to himself.

***

"Where is Onome?" Mama Onome asked Edirin.

"I don't know," Edirin answered. "The last time I set my eyes on him was yesterday morning."

Panic suffused her face; she was alarmed by Edirin's answer. She went outside to meet her husband.

Since the disappearance of his car, Pa Efe had been acting strangely. He wore the look of someone whose world had fallen apart. His world had indeed crumbled. The car was his most prized possession.

"Pa Onome, have you seen Onome today?"

"No," he answered curtly.

"Onome did not sleep in this house yesterday. I'm beginning to get worried about his whereabouts."

"Look woman, what do you want me to do? He is a grown up and old enough to take care of himself. Please don't disturb me again, allow me to think about my stolen car."

"Papa Onome, your son's whereabouts is

shrouded in mystery. Onome has never slept outside before. We have cause to be worried. Which is more important, your old jalopy or Onome?"

"Will you shut up woman, you call my 504 GL 1982 model a jalopy? I don't blame you, none of your brothers can afford to buy a car. The only means of transportation your elder brother could afford was a bicycle. Look woman, don't make me vent my annoyance on you," Pa Efe said, fuming.

"Shameless man, if you are not concerned, I am! I will go and look for him." She went inside to change her dress.

Mama Onome combed the whole area in search of Onome.

A neighbour suggested that they visit the morgues in Lagos because one could find a missing relation in there. She also reported his disappearance to the police.

One week after Onome's disappearance, Pa Efe became worried. Onome had never left home without telling anyone where he was going.

Three weeks after Onome's disappearance,

the postman delivered a letter addressed to Pa Efe.

"Edirin! Edirin! Bring my glasses," Pa Efe shouted. He opened the letter.

Edirin brought his glasses.

"Papa is it my admission letter?" he asked anxiously.

"No," Pa Efe snapped. He put on his glasses and began to read the letter.

Dear Papa,

First, I must apologise for causing you and mum undue anxiety. Forgive me for not writing since I left home unceremoniously. I would have written since, but due to some minor but important problems I couldn't.

Papa, I must confess that I sold your car to get money. This may shock you, but I had to do it.

As you can see from the address above, I am writing from London. I sold your car to buy my ticket to London. A friend of mine gave me two hundred and sixty thousand naira. I needed three hundred thousand naira for my trip and I had no choice but to sell your car to complete the money.

I am really sorry Dad, what I did was for the benefit of the family. I had no other option than to leave the country to search of the Golden Fleece overseas.

I've got a job now; I work in a restaurant as a waiter. The salary is okay. I'm still searching for another job. If I get one, I'll be earning double my present salary. As soon as I make enough money, I'll send some down, at least to alleviate the suffering of the family. But rest assured that when I come home, I'll buy you another car.

Greetings to Mama, and my younger brothers and sisters.

Onome

Pa Efe dropped the letter. He was furious. "So Onome has the audacity to tell me that he sold my car to better the lot of the family!" he said to no one in particular. "That useless son of his mother must have connived with his mother... Mama Onome! Mama Onome!"

"Yes!" she answered from inside.

"Come here at once, I've got news for you."

She came out of the room.

"Yes, Papa Onome, what is the news? Have

they found Onome? Did the police pass any information to you?" she asked anxiously.

"I've just received a letter from that … I mean from your son, Onome."

"Hey! Onome! Praise the Lord!"

"Woman, let me finish before you start shouting." He paused to make sure his words sank in. "Onome wrote from London."

"London? What is he doing there? And how is he?"

"He is fine," Pa Efe said.

"Oh, we thank God o," Mama Onome broke into a song.

Pa Efe looked at her disdainfully.

"Anyway, that is not the reason I called you. I called you tell you that I've found the thief who stole my car."

"Where? Who is he?" Mama Onome asked.

"Where? Who is he?" Pa Efe mimicked. "Look at her pretending. You think I don't know that you know the identity of the thief," he said sarcastically.

"What do you mean, Papa Onome?" Mama Onome said, getting angry.

"Don't tell me you didn't plan with Onome to steal my car!"

"Your car? You mean Onome was the person that stole your car?"

"Yes, he sold it to get money to go to London."

Mama Onome began to weep.

"Look woman, you cannot fool me with your crocodile tears. I am certain that you connived with your son to steal my car."

"Papa Onome, that is a cruel thing to say…"

"Look who's talking about cruelty, when you connived with your son to steal my car you didn't know it was cruel, abi? Yeye woman, Onome behaves exactly like your wayward brother…"

"Papa Onome, please leave my elder brother out of this."

"Shut up Mama Onome, I say shut up! Now will you get out of my sight before I lose my temper? I have a good mind to send you packing."

Pa Efe was bluffing when he threatened to send Mama Onome packing. He knew he could not send her away because she was the breadwinner of the family. He was also certain that she had no hand in the theft of his car. He accused her simply because he wanted to vent his spleen and frustration on her.

***

A car pulled up in front of the Badmus residence. A tall, young man alighted from the car, a BMW 5 series. He walked up to the gate and rang the bell.

The young man was dressed in a nicely fitted suit. He was bespectacled.

"Yes? Na who you dey look for?" the gateman asked.

"Abeg Madam Tinuke dey house? Na she I dey look for," the young man answered.

"Na who you be? She dey expect you?"

"No, I just wan surprise am with dis visit. I be im very good friend, you mean say you no recognize me?" The young man asked the gateman. He took off his glasses.

The gateman took a closer look at him; a flicker of recognition crossed his face.

"Madam dey inside, ah Oga sorry o, I no know say na you. You know say e don tey since I see you."

"No problem, my friend, I no blame you. I know say di glasses wey I knack for face been confuse you."

"Na true you talk Oga."

The young man was ushered into the living room by the steward. Not long after, Tinuke walked in. She was dressed in khaki shorts and a white T-shirt. She recognized the young man instantly. She ran into his outstretched arms. Tears of joy cascaded down her cheeks. They clung tightly to each other for what seemed like eternity before they finally broke their embrace.

"Onome I am really delighted to see you again, why didn't you write to tell me you were coming home? I can see you have filled out, seem taller and still as handsome as ever. Welcome back to Nigeria my darling. I missed you," Tinuke said, beaming with smiles.

"Tinu my baby, you're looking lovely. Please forgive me for not writing often or informing you of my visit. I wanted to surprise you. I missed you too, just two years and it's as if I've been separated from you for ages."

"When did you arrive?"

"Yesterday."

"Oh Onome, it's a pleasure to see you again."

Tinuke was very happy that Onome was back at last. Her parents were mounting pressure on her to marry Ade. Her mother kept on reminding her of her age. She was just twenty-four, but she realized that she was not getting any younger. Despite the pressure from her parents, she had vowed to wait for Onome. Whether her parents liked it or not she would marry the love of her life.

Onome gave her a blow-by-blow account of how he had fared in London. His few letters had been brief and without much detail.

"You mean you kept three jobs?" Tinuke asked when Onome finished his narration.

"Yes my dear, it wasn't easy. I had to because of you and my family. Tinu, I'll never leave you again. I'll always be right there by your side. I have a gift for you."

He brought out a small box from his pocket and gave it to her.

"Open it."

She opened it. "Wow!" she exclaimed,

admiring the diamond necklace in the box. She brought it out and tried it on. "This must have cost you a fortune."

"It's actually nothing, this is just a token of my love," Onome said.

"Oh Onome, thanks, it's so beautiful!" She wrapped her arms round him and kissed him full on the lips.

***

Mama! Mama! Mama! Guess who's here!" Edirin shouted, running out to meet the young man who alighted from the BMW 5 series.

"What is it Edirin? Why are you shouting like someone chased by masquerades?" Mama Onome said, coming out of the room to see what was amiss.

"Onome! Onome! Onome!" She rushed to embrace him. They hugged each other tightly. Edirin carried some of his brother's luggage inside.

"Welcome my son, welcome! Look at you! London is really good o."

Mama Onome was elated to see her son. Two years had seemed like ages to her. They went in together.

From inside, Pa Efe heard the noise, but he couldn't leave to find out what it was all about because he was presiding over the monthly family meeting with his brothers.

"Digwo," Onome greeted in Isoko dialect when he entered the sitting room, his elated mother by his side.

"Vredo," his uncles chorused.

"Welcome back, my son," Edoja, Pa Efe's immediate younger brother said. "How was your trip?" he asked.

"It was fine, sir," Onome answered.

Pa Efe did not say a word. He glared at Onome. He ignored Onome when he greeted. A knife could have cut through the tension in the air.

"My son, let's go inside." His mother dragged Onome into the bedroom.

"Brother, I know how angry you were when you found out that Onome had sold your car, but by now you should be happy that he is back, hale and hearty and apparently made good," ventured Edoja. "Let's rejoice and forget the past. It is time to bury the hatchet. I am sure he regrets his action." Edoja paused to look round the room to see if his brothers were in support, and from the expression in their eyes he knew they were. "Brother, please for our sake forgive your son, let bygones be bygones."

"Brother, we agree with Edoja," Pa Efe's six brothers chorused.

"My brothers, I thank all of you for your concern. Edoja, you have spoken well. I'll talk to my son later, please let us continue with our meeting," Pa Efe said.

Meanwhile, in the bedroom Onome showed his mother and siblings the gifts he had brought for them.

"Mama, we've escaped poverty," Onome said. "From now on, we will no longer live from hand to mouth. Very soon we shall move into another house."

Mama Onome's joy knew no bounds. She started singing.

He has done for me,
He has done for me,
What my husband cannot do,
He has done for me.

"Will you shut up woman!" Pa Efe shouted from the sitting room, annoyed.

"Papa Onome, what is the matter, aren't you happy that your son is back?" Mama Onome asked.

"Yes, I know I will not have peace in my own house because your wayward son is back," Pa Efe retorted.

"Papa, please forgive Onome," Oke said.

"Will you shut up!" Pa Efe shouted angrily. "Oh, oh I see, like mother like daughter."

He stood up and left the room.

Onome, who was within earshot, came out of the bedroom.

"Don't worry Mama, I know what to do. By tomorrow Papa will get over his anger."

The next day Onome went to buy a "Tokunbo" Mercedes Benz 200 for his dad.

Pa Efe, who had been seating outside, was dumbfounded when he saw Onome alight from the Benz.

Onome went straight to his father and knelt down: "Papa I have come to apologise for what I did. I am very sorry. Please accept the keys to the Benz. It is yours."

A smile lit up Pa Efe's face. "Onome, Onome, you mean that car parked there is for me?"

"Yes Papa."

"Onome, Onomsky, you are really my own, I have always said it, that you are a blessing. You are really my offspring. The true son of Efe Oghale. Get up my son."

Onome got up. They went to inspect the car. The car, painted white, sparkled in the sun. It was a used car imported into the country from Germany, and in very good condition, grade one as described in street slang.

"Papa Onome, who is the owner of this car"? Mama Onome asked, coming to join them outside when she saw Onome with his father.

"It is mine," Pa Efe answered happily.

"Yours?"

"Yes, mine, Onome bought it for me."

"Praise the Lord! We now have a car; neighbours come and praise the Lord with me o!" Mama Onome shouted. She danced round the car.

Some of the tenants came out to find out what was going on. They were attracted by Mama Onome's shouting.

"Papa Onome, we go wash de car o," one of them said. They were all in a joyous mood.

Pa Efe could not hide his joy and gratitude. He puts his arms around Onome.

"Onome, God bless you, thank you very much."

"Oh Papa, don't mention, the car is just a tip of the iceberg. I have other good things in store for you," Onome said.

Onome and his dad went inside.

"Lest I forget, Papa, I bought some pairs of shoes and suits for you."

Onome brought out the shoes and suits from a suitcase. He gave them to his dad.

"You mean these are for me?"

"Yes, Papa."

"Onome, I am grateful. You see, I knew you would someday better our lot. Even when you left unceremoniously, I didn't lose hope. I told your mother that the people who advised me to disown you for stealing my car were all enemies of progress and..."

"Papa Onome, Papa Onome, stop lying," Mama Onome interjected. "Have you forgotten the abuses, you rained on me, you blamed me for Onome's misconduct. Your brothers called me names. They even advised you to throw me out. Which you almost did, if not for the fact that you realised that if I leave, you'll starve to death..."

"Mama, let bygones be bygones. Forget whatever Papa said in the past. Let us rejoice and not quarrel" Onome said.

"Thank you, my son, you are really my offspring. Did I ever tell you that your grandfather was an orator? I can see that you've inherited his gift of oratory and, my dear," Papa Onome pulled Mama Onome closer, "I am sorry for all the pains I put you through, forgive me for all the unsavoury things I said about you in the past. Let's give peace a chance, at least for Onome's sake."

The Oghales moved into a new house in Dolphin Estate, Ikoyi.

Five months later, Onome married Tinuke. Dr Badmus finally gave his blessing to the union.

"Wow!" we all screamed after Dr Ifeka had finished reading from his younger brother's manuscript.

"Any questions, comments?" he asked us and adjusted his reading glasses. Many hands shot up. Dr Ifeka's Literary Criticism class was our favourite class. We looked forward to it because he had a way of making his lectures very interesting and encouraged us to ask questions. Little wonder he was the most liked lecturer in the English Language department.

"Yes, Sade, what is your question?" I knew he was going to pick on me. He had the habit of picking students whose hands were not up. As usual, I had kept my hands down. It wasn't as if I didn't have any question to ask, but I was a bit on the shy side and found it difficult standing to ask questions in class. I stood up shyly and, in a voice I could barely recognize as my own, I asked, "is the story based on a true-life account sir?"

Before Dr Ifeka could answer the question, the bell buzzed, signalling the end of his period.

"Oh no!" the whole class chorused, disappointed that the lecture was over.

I had asked a question that was on everybody's mind and, from all indications, we would have to wait till next week to find out if Dr Ifeka's story was fact or fiction or a bit of both.

Sam Umukoro is an award winning journalist and writer. He has written for the Vanguard and Guardian newspapers in Nigeria . Once Upon A Monday is his first collection of short stories .

Printed in Great Britain
by Amazon

67485351R00076